THE TEAM

UP AND RUNNING

Written by Alan Durant
Illustrated by Maggie Roman

Thanks to Inclusive Minds (the CIC supporting and championing inclusion and diversity in children's books) for introducing us to Kay and Gabriella through their network of Inclusion Ambassadors.

Special thanks also to Harrison, Parker and Reegan.

30131 05806572 0

LONDON BOROUGH OF BARNET

Titles in the Making the Team Series:

The Challenge

The Battle

Up and Running

Paying the Penalty

Taking a Stand

The Final

Badger Publishing Limited
Oldmedow Road,
Hardwick Industrial Estate,
King's Lynn PE30 4JJ

Telephone: **01553 816 082**
www.badgerlearning.co.uk

2 4 6 8 10 9 7 5 3

Up and Running
ISBN 978-1-78837-657-0

Text © Alan Durant 2022
Illustration © Maggie Roman 2022
Complete work © Badger Publishing Limited 2022

All rights reserved. No part of this publication may be reproduced,
stored in any form or by any means mechanical, electronic, recording
or otherwise without the prior permission of the publisher.

The right of Alan Durant to be identified as author of
this Work has been asserted by him in accordance with the Copyright,
Designs and Patents Act 1988.

Commissioning Editor: Sarah Rudd
Editor: Claire Morgan
Designer: Bigtop Design
Cover: alphaspirit.it/Shutterstock

UP AND RUNNING

Contents

Characters

Ron Grant

Alex Cook (Cookie)

Callum

Jorge Alvarez

Angelo

Jackson

Mani Gronier

Jadon Brooks

Bradley

Marissa

Vocabulary

back four: the defensive team members in a football team

channels: the spaces between a center back and full back

debut: playing the first ever game for a team

digs: a place to stay or live

set plays: planned tactics during either a free kick or a corner kick

stepovers: raising the foot over the top of the ball to trick an opposing player

superstitions: a belief that is not based on science or reason, usually associated with the supernatural

tapes: used to keep shin pads in place

CHAPTER ONE

"Rise and shine, Callum! You've got a big day ahead," said Callum's mum as she drew back the curtains.

Today was the biggest day in the whole of Callum's seventeen years of life. It was the first match in the Cathay Cup, a pre-season tournament hosted by Premier League team Stanford FC. It featured some of the biggest clubs in Europe. And Callum was in the Stanford squad for the first time ever!

Okay, he was only on the bench, but five subs were allowed and the manager Ron Grant said he planned to use them all.

The tournament format was simple: two groups of four teams with the winners going on to play the final. Stanford's first match was against Spanish side Sevilla and Callum couldn't wait.

"Did you sleep all right?" Mum asked.

Callum yawned as if on cue. "I couldn't get to sleep for ages," he said. "I was too excited."

Lying in bed, he had imagined lots of ways the game might go. They all ended with him coming onto the pitch and scoring the winning goal.

"Well, jump in the shower and I'll make you breakfast," Mum said.

In the shower, Callum thought back to just over a week ago when Ron Grant had called him and four other young players from the Under-21 team to his office.

Grant had given them a challenge. He said they could train with the First Team and, if they impressed him, they would be part of the squad for the Cathay Cup.

Callum hadn't had the best week, but somehow, he'd made it through with two of the others, Jackson and Angelo.

Ten minutes later, dried and dressed, Callum sat at the kitchen table eating scrambled eggs on toast, followed by a banana and a glass of fresh orange juice. Usually he wolfed down his breakfast but today he had to force himself to eat. He felt shaky with nerves.

"Good luck, my brilliant boy," Mum said with a smile, as Callum opened the front door. She kissed him on the cheek. "Score a goal for me."

Callum returned her smile, nervously. "I'll do my best, Mum. If I even get on the pitch."

Callum was glad it was only a five-minute walk from his house to the Cathay arena, Stanford FC's home ground. He needed to be with other people to keep him distracted from the upcoming game.

In the car park, Callum met up with Jackson who was coming from his digs. They grinned and slapped hands.

"How you feeling, mate?" Jackson asked.

"Good," Callum replied, trying to hide his nerves. "Excited."

Jackson nodded. "Me too."

Jackson was in the starting lineup for the first time. He was taking the place of Mani Gronier, one of Stanford's biggest stars.

"You'll be great," Callum said. He really meant it.

Jackson was only six months older than Callum, but he seemed so grown up. He was the captain of the Under-21s and Callum had never seen him have a bad game.

"I hope so," Jackson said with a shaky sigh.

Even Jackson, who always seemed so cool and calm, had nerves.

"Are your family coming to watch?" Callum asked.

"Marissa is," Jackson replied.

Marissa was Jackson's sister. She was part of the Stanford women's team.

"My dad is working. My mum hopes she can change her shift at the supermarket. What about you?" asked Jackson.

"My mum is coming," Callum replied.

Callum didn't want to talk about his dad, so he changed the subject and suggested going to the gym.

CHAPTER TWO

Callum and Jackson spent an hour in the gym. Callum had set himself a strict routine of exercises over the last couple of weeks. He was trying to improve his upper-body strength and his stamina. But today, they just had a gentle workout: some stretches, sit-ups and a couple of short stints on the exercise bike. They didn't want to tire themselves out before the match.

Afterwards, they went to the players' lounge. Most of the team were there. Some were sitting on the sofas chatting. A small group were having a game of cards. Jadon Brooks and Jorge Alvarez were playing pool.

Angelo was on his own listening to his iPad. He looked terrified. Callum went over and patted him on the shoulder.

Angelo jumped but he smiled when he saw it was Callum. He took out his earphones.

"Where have you been? I thought you weren't coming," Angelo said anxiously.

"Not coming? To the biggest event of our lives?" Callum questioned, laughing.

"We've been in the gym," Jackson explained.

"Any of you lads fancy a game of pool?" called Brooks. "I'm tired of beating Jorge."

Callum shrugged. "Yeah, I'll give it a go," he offered.

He wasn't the best pool player, but it would pass the time and help him hide his nerves.

Jadon was too good for Callum and for Jackson too, when he played him next. Angelo did the best. He actually won a game against Brooks, gaining a nod of respect from the captain.

A little while later, Ron Grant and First Team coach, Alex Cook, came in and gave a quick recap talk about the tournament. Then they showed some clips of Sevilla on the big screen.

"They're dangerous at set plays, so keep your wits about you," Cookie warned.

Grant insisted that the whole matchday squad ate lunch together. They all sat down at one long table.

Callum wasn't that hungry, but he had some pasta. Angelo had the same. Jackson tucked in to a plate piled with chicken and rice with vegetables.

"You love your food, don't you?" Callum laughed.

"My engine needs a lot of fuel," Jackson replied.

It was true. The players needed a lot of energy if they were going to beat Sevilla, especially Jackson, who had to constantly run from one end of the pitch to the other.

It seemed to Callum as if time was barely moving. He just wanted to get out on the pitch and kick a ball around.

Some of the players made jokes and fooled around, but Callum couldn't join in. He wondered how they could be so relaxed before such a big game. But then, many of them were internationals, used to playing big matches every week. This was his first time.

The first of many, he hoped...

CHAPTER THREE

An hour before kick-off, the players started to go down to the changing room to get ready. When he pushed the door open, Callum looked around in awe.

All the shirts of the players were hanging up above the bench, waiting for their owners. And there it was:

COOPER 19.

Callum's heart did a flip.

When Callum was a child, he had a replica shirt with the name and number of his hero on the back. He still had it at home. ALVAREZ 10. It was his favourite.

And now he, Callum Cooper, had a real Stanford shirt with his name on it. Plus, he was going to sit on the First Team bench with his hero beside him.

He couldn't believe it.

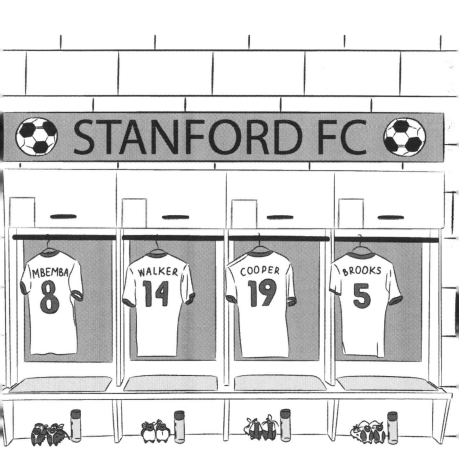

Callum took his time getting into his kit. He wanted to enjoy every moment.

He put the socks and shorts on and then his training top. He took the shirt down and put it over his lap, name up, so that he could just gaze at it. It was the most beautiful thing he had ever seen. Callum would remember this moment forever.

Callum's best friend, Bradley, was Stanford's biggest fan and he came to every match. He was so excited when Callum passed the manager's challenge and was picked for the First Team squad.

Bradley knew all about the players and their ways, much more than Callum did. He told Callum to look out for some of their habits and superstitions.

For example, Jadon Brooks always put his left shin pad on first and tied the tapes around his socks three times. Well, Callum watched him, and Bradley was right.

One of the most superstitious players was Mani Gronier, who usually played in centre midfield. He had to be the last person to tie up his boot laces and the last to go onto the pitch.

Once, when the team went out after half-time, one of the players was still getting some treatment and Gronier refused to leave the changing room. In the end, both players missed the restart and Gronier was booked by the ref for coming onto the pitch before there was a break in play.

That wouldn't happen today, though, because Gronier had been banned by the manager for one game for starting a fight in training. Jackson was taking his place.

Before the players went out for their warm-up, Ron Grant came into the changing room to give his team talk.

"Right, lads. You know all about Sevilla and what a top side they are, so you'll need to be at it from the kick-off. I want a fast start.

"Put them under pressure straight away and see if they crack. Their last big match was the UEFA League final, which they lost. They might still be feeling uneasy from that, so let's hit them hard.

"Brooks, I want you to keep the defensive line high. But don't let their central striker, Gomez, run in behind. He's lightning fast and you'll never catch him.

"Jackson, I know it's your first game but I want you to protect the back four with your life. Understand me?"

"Yes, boss," Jackson nodded.

"We've got a full bench and I'll be making changes today," Grant continued. "If you feel any muscle pulls or twinges I want you off, okay? We've got a long season ahead."

He put his hand on his hips and gave his players the famous Grant glare. "Right, now, get out there and win."

CHAPTER FOUR

Callum sat in his seat between Angelo and Jorge Alvarez, behind Ron Grant and Alex Cook.

Callum had felt great warming up in front of a crowd, hearing the fans' cheers when he walked out with the other subs for the very first time. The Cathay arena was still filling up at the time, but the atmosphere was already enough to send a tingle down Callum's spine.

But the roar when the team strode out for the kick-off was something else. Wow!

Glancing to his left, Callum could see Bradley, wearing his Stanford FC shirt, sitting in his wheelchair at the front of the west stand.

Callum's mum was here too, but higher up with the families of the other players, so he couldn't see her. It was good though, knowing she was here.

For a moment, as the players lined up for the kick-off, Callum thought of his dad.

This had been his dad's dream too, to play for Stanford FC, his hometown club. It would have been nice if he could have been here, but he never watched football anymore. The injuries that had ended his football career at nineteen had left him bitter and angry. He'd walked out a year ago and Callum hadn't seen him since.

Both sides took the knee to show they were against racism. Then, with another roar from the crowd, Stanford kicked off.

They began well, just as Grant had ordered. Their passing was slick and sharp and they didn't let Sevilla settle.

Jadon Brooks got close with a header from a corner. Then the Sevilla keeper saved a stinging shot from striker, Reegan Keller, Stanford's new signing. Keller had another chance too and he should have scored, but the ball went wide from six-yards out.

Callum groaned with the fans. He was sure that he would have scored. If only he was playing.

After their shaky start, Sevilla started to get into the match. They had a clever Brazilian playmaker, Melo, who was always finding space. Twice, his searching passes nearly set up Sevilla's quick striker, Gomez, to score, but Stanford's defence held and caught him offside. The manager's plan was working.

But, for Stanford, it was third time unlucky.

Once more, Melo slid the ball into space behind the Stanford defence and Gomez was onto it in a flash.

Brooks held up his hand, hoping for the
linesman to flag for offside, but this time
Gomez had timed his run to perfection.
He showed his speed as he sprinted forwards
and then slipped the ball under the goalie
and into the net.

1-0 to Sevilla.

Callum and Angelo turned to each other, both looking frustrated. This wasn't how they had imagined the game going.

The goal seemed to affect Stanford's rhythm. Their passing lost its energy and they couldn't make any chances. Time after time, moves broke down in the final third of the pitch.

The crowd became restless. Instead of cheers, there were groans.

At least Jackson was doing okay. He was one of the few players whose playing level stayed high. He made a great tackle in the last minute of the first half to stop Melo having a clear shot at a goal.

The ref's whistle blew for half-time. Ron Grant stood up quickly and marched towards the tunnel. Callum, Angelo and the other subs followed him. What would Grant say?

CHAPTER FIVE

Ron Grant was not happy. His half-time team talk was angry. He grunted and swore and called his team 'sloppy'.

"You look as if you're still on your summer holidays," he growled. "You're lucky to only be one goal down. You have got to do better in the second half."

Grant told Jorge Alvarez to strip off because he was coming on for Keller.

"We need to get back into this match fast," he said. "I want to see a hundred percent effort. No, a hundred and ten percent. Get the crowd behind you."

When the team went out for the second half, Cookie told Callum and Angelo to warm up.

Callum's heart leapt. Was he really going to come on?

Callum did a few stretches, then jogged up and down the line, while keeping an eye on the game.

It was very even with both defences working hard. Neither side was making any chances. Stanford were looking weak up front.

Cookie waved to Callum and Angelo to come back to the bench.

"Shirts and shin pads on, lads," he said. "You're coming on."

Callum went back to his seat where his shirt was waiting for him. He picked it up and kissed the badge before swapping it for his training top. He slipped his shin pads inside his socks and put on the ties. Then he stood up and walked down to the technical area.

This was it. It was time to show the world what he could do.

Cookie held up an iPad with a diagram showing where and how he wanted Callum to play.

"You've got pace. Run the channels. But if it goes out wide, make sure you're in the centre," he instructed. "We need a goal."

Callum nodded, but he couldn't really take in the coach's words. All he could think about was that he was going to take to the pitch to make his debut in the Stanford First Team.

Angelo stood next to Callum on the touchline. He looked more scared than excited.

"Good luck," Callum said.

"You too," Angelo nodded.

Ron Grant turned and gazed at Callum. "Give us a goal, son. I'm relying on you."

Next time the ball went out of play, the fourth official put up his board for the substitutions. Callum shook hands briefly with the player coming off, then trotted onto the pitch.

The clapping of the crowd gave him goosebumps. Hardly any of them had seen him play, yet still they were welcoming him. He couldn't let them down.

Callum's first couple of touches were poor.

He failed to receive a pass cleanly and a pass of his own ended up with the other side.

Jorge Alvarez jogged past him, muttering, "Settle down. Take your time."

Callum took a deep breath and began to feel calmer. The next time the ball came his way he controlled it instantly and flicked it wide to Angelo, who went on a run that won a corner.

Angelo may have looked totally terrified when he was off the pitch waiting, but once he was on and had the ball at his feet, he didn't appear to be nervous at all.

Angelo took the corner and the Sevilla defence cleared the ball, but Jackson swept it up and passed it out to Angelo again. A couple of stepovers and he was past the opposing full back.

Angelo sent a wicked cross towards the goal. Callum's eyes lit up as he met the ball perfectly with his head. It had to be a goal.

But, no!

Somehow the Sevilla goalie got a fingertip to the ball and tipped it on to the post. Callum grimaced. The crowd groaned.

The near miss changed the mood in the arena. The crowd was noisier, cheering Stanford on.

Once again, Jackson won the ball in midfield. He sprinted forwards, then passed to Callum.

Without thinking, Callum played the ball back to Jackson. Jackson slipped the ball between two defenders and Angelo was on to it, racing to the byline before cutting the ball back to the edge of the six-yard box.

Jorge Alvarez was there to guide the ball coolly into the corner of the net.

Stanford were level!

For the rest of the match, Stanford were on top, but they couldn't get the goal their attacking play deserved.

Ron Grant was a lot happier at the end than he had been at half-time. He shook every player's hand.

"Well done, son," Grant said to Callum, as he walked off the pitch. "You didn't score, but you did okay."

Callum knew this was high praise indeed, coming from Grant.

He looked across the pitch and saw Bradley giving him a thumbs up. He grinned and raised his own thumb in reply. They would have a lot to talk about later. But for now he was going to enjoy the atmosphere in the changing room.

They hadn't won, but, more importantly, they hadn't lost. There was still all to play for, and what's more, Callum had played a part in the equalising goal.

Like the team, he was up and running!

Further activities

1 Ron Grant insists that the squad all sit down and eat lunch together on matchday. Create a healthy and balanced meal plan that a footballer could follow on matchday.

2 Callum's heart did a flip when he saw his football shirt for the first time. Design a football shirt that you would like to wear. Don't forget to include the club logo!

Further resources

The history of taking the knee against racism began with Martin Luther King and the American civil rights movement. Since 2020, it has been used in sports events to highlight the issues of racism still present in society today.

Learn more here:
www.bbc.co.uk/news/explainers-53098516

Also, visit **www.theredcard.org** to learn about the UK's leading anti-racism educational charity, Show Racism the Red Card.

Enjoyed this book?

Follow the Making the Team journey
across all six brilliant stories!

badgerlearning.co.uk @badgerlearning